MARY STANLEY

BRUNO, PEANUT AND ME

Mary Stanley has published six novels: *Retreat* (2001), *Missing* (2002), *Revenge* (2004), *Searching for Home* (2005), *The Lost Garden* (2006) and *The Umbrella Tree* (2009). In 2008, she published a novella, *An Angel at My Back* in the Open Door series. Mary currently lives in Dublin. See www.marystanley.com. All royalties from the Irish sales of the Open Door series go to a charity of the author's choice. *Bruno, Peanut and Me* royalties go to The Dublin Rape Crisis Centre, 70 Lower Leeson Street, Dublin 2.

NEW ISLAND *Open Door*

BRUNO, PEANUT AND ME
First published 2011
by New Island
2 Brookside
Dundrum Road
Dublin 14
www.newisland.ie

A CIP catalogue record for this book is available from the British Library

ISBN 978-1-84840-103-7

New Island receives financial assistance from The Arts Council (An
Chomhairle Ealaíon), Dublin, Ireland.

Typeset by Mariel Deegan
Printed by Drukarnia Skleniarz
Cover design by Artmark

10 9 8 7 6 5 4 3 2 1

Dear Reader,

On behalf of myself and the other contributing authors, I would like to welcome you to the seventh Open Door series. We hope that you enjoy the books and that reading becomes a lasting pleasure in your life.

Warmest wishes,

Patricia Scanlan.

Patricia Scanlan
Series Editor

THE OPEN DOOR SERIES IS DEVELOPED WITH THE ASSISTANCE OF THE CITY OF DUBLIN VOCATIONAL EDUCATION COMMITTEE.

For Doreen

CHAPTER ONE

Bruno Little was one year older than me. He had dark brown hair, brown eyes and a straight nose. Everyone said he was a lovely looking boy. When I was born he was one year old. When I was one, he was two. The years passed, and when I was seven, he was eight.

Bruno Little was the funniest, cleverest and happiest person I have ever met. He was also the meanest.

People used to say, "What a charming child." Bruno always smiled sweetly when people said nice things about him. He had the nicest face and lovely skin. His lips opened into a wonderful smile. He looked lovely.

But you can be lovely on the outside and not so nice on the inside. And I should know.

Bruno Little was my brother.

My name is Susan, but everyone calls me Susie. Bruno and I have a little sister called Peanut.

Her real name is Penny. But when she was born Bruno called her Peanut and the name stuck. He tried to call me Wart. In fact he did call me Wart, but the name did not stick for anyone other than him. I do not like being called Wart. A wart is a virus thing on your skin.

My Dad said to Bruno, "Bruno, don't call her Wart. It's not nice."

Bruno said, "I'm calling her that after a warthog. I like warthogs."

My Dad said, "Oh, I see."

I think being named after a warthog is worse than being named after a wart, but Dad did not see it that way.

"Oh, I see," Dad said again. "Warthogs are interesting animals."

"Very interesting," Bruno said. "I read about them. They are called warthogs because they have four tusks that look like warts."

"Dad," I yelled. "I don't have tusks."

"Of course you don't," Dad said. "You have very nice teeth."

When Dad went out of the room, Bruno said to me, "Warthogs are the ugliest animals. Look in the mirror, Wart, and then look in my book on animals. There is a photo of you in my book."

He said that when Dad was not listening.

He said horrible things when no one else was around.

I looked in his book.

A warthog was a very ugly pig with huge tusks.

Peanut was two years younger than me. She worried about little things. In fact she worried about everything. One of the reasons she worried was because of Bruno. She had reason to worry, but not as much reason as me.

When I was three years old, Bruno got my Dad's penknife and he stuck it in my hand.

I screamed and screamed.

Mum said, "Susie, what have you done?"

"I didn't do it," I sobbed. "Bruno did it." Did she really think I had stabbed myself? Did she really think I was that stupid?

"Bruno, why did you do that?" Mum asked him as she washed my hand and held it in a towel.

"I didn't mean to," Bruno said. "Oh, poor little Susie. I didn't mean to hurt her."

"You must not play with knives," Mum said to him as she put the knife up high on a shelf.

Peanut was too little to remember that, but she was there when Bruno tried to set fire to my new green dress.

My dress was apple green. It had a dark green satin ribbon that went around my waist and tied in a big bow at the back. It was my birthday. There was a big chocolate cake on the table with seven candles on it. I was looking at my cake with Peanut beside me.

"Nice cake," Peanut said.

I nodded. I was so excited. It was a lovely cake. Mum had made it. There were little purple sugared violets on it and my seven pink candles. It was the nicest cake I had ever seen.

Bruno came into the room with a box of matches.

"Susie's cake is beautiful," Peanut said. She had big brown eyes just like Bruno. She was staring at the cake with her eyes wide open.

"Hah," said Bruno as he lit a match.

"Bruno, you can't," I said. "We're not lighting the candles until later when my school friends come for my party."

"Hah," said Bruno as he came towards me with his match lighting. With one hand he held my arm, and with the other he tried to light my dress.

I screamed and screamed.

Peanut fell into my chocolate birthday cake and the match fell on to the floor.

"Look what you've done," Bruno said.

My apple green dress had a scorch mark on it.

My chocolate cake was ruined.

Peanut had chocolate on her face and little sugared violets in her hair. Bruno said to me, "You should not play with matches, Wart."

"I didn't," I shouted.

"You did," Bruno said. "You saw her, Peanut. You saw her lighting the match."

Peanut shook her head. She was trying to shake some of the chocolate off her face.

"You did, Peanut. You did," Bruno said.

"Yes," said Peanut.

Mum came into the room. She was shocked at the state of the cake and at the state of my dress. I was sent to my room to change out of it. She told me to put on my school clothes.

"But it's my birthday party," I said.

"I don't care," Mum said. "You should not touch matches. Look at what you've done, Susie."

"I didn't do it. Peanut, tell her," I shouted.

But Peanut was afraid to tell her.

Peanut was afraid of Bruno.

So was I.

I spent my seventh birthday in my school clothes: my grey skirt, white shirt and blue jumper. I had no birthday cake. And I hated Bruno with all my heart.

CHAPTER TWO

We lived in a house by the sea.

From the windows in our house we could see the railway line, a high wall and then the sea. In the summer we swam and played in the water.

In the winter we watched the sea going in and out, pulling back across the sand until it almost disappeared, then slowly washing in again until all the rocks were under water.

In spring, the tides were so high they splashed over the wall and on to the railway track.

"Hah," said Bruno. "I wonder will it keep coming in, until the tracks are covered and it comes right up to our house."

"Oh, no," said Peanut, with one more thing to worry about. "What will happen then?"

"We'll be flooded and we'll be washed away," said Bruno, happily.

"Oh, no," repeated Peanut.

"Don't worry, Peanut," I said to my little sister. "We'll get an ark and sail away, like Noah did."

"Noah put two of each animal on the ark," said Bruno. "Well, we'll only need to get one more warthog."

I bit my lip. I wanted to hit him. I wanted to push him out the window.

He grinned at me. "We could live in a submarine," he said. "A yellow one, like in the song."

The three of us sang together, "*We all live in a yellow submarine…*"

But then Bruno laughed and said it was a very small submarine and there would not be room for me.

So then I hit him.

I hit him hard and he fell over. He lay on the floor and he didn't move. His eyes were closed.

I got such a fright as I thought I had killed him. I bent down to look closer at his face and he grabbed my hair and pulled it very hard.

"I will tell Mum what you did," Bruno said as I tried to get free. "I am telling on you and they'll send you away."

I pulled away from him and I ran to my bedroom.

I had my own bedroom. Sort of. It was a big room with a large window that looked out over the garden and the railway line and the sea. Down the middle of the room was a pink curtain. I had my bed on one side. Peanut's bed was on the other.

Peanut was very tidy. Her clothes were always tidied away. Her slippers were on the floor beside her bed, and her teddy bear lay on the pillow.

Her side was nicer than mine. I could only ever find one of my slippers. I never seemed to have the two at any one time. My clothes were on the floor and my bed was not made.

The light beside my bed did not work as I had knocked it over and the bulb had blown.

I climbed on to Peanut's bed and I hugged her teddy bear.

Some days I just hated myself. This was one of those days.

Mum came into the room.

"Get off Peanut's bed," she said. "And go to your own bed and stay there. How many times have I told you not to fight with Bruno?" She stood there with her hands on her hips and a cross look on her face.

I didn't know whether to answer her or not. I didn't know how many times she had told me not to fight with Bruno. Hundreds, I suppose.

"I'm sorry," I said.

"Go to your own bed," she repeated. "And stay there. I'm stopping your pocket money and you can just stay in your room until you learn how to behave."

I went to bed.

I hated them all.

I hated Bruno because he was so mean.

And I hated Mum because she didn't see it.

And I hated Peanut because she could have told Mum that I hadn't started the fight.

And I hated Dad because he would take Mum's side when he got home and I would get no pocket money.

And most of all I hated me.

I hated the fact that I had let Bruno upset me. I knew he had caused the fight, but I also knew that I could have walked away. After all, there would be no ark and no submarine, so we were fighting about something that was never going to happen.

I lay on my bed and I thought about everything. I thought about how I could not change other people, but that maybe, just maybe, I could change myself.

In the mess on the floor beside my bed I found my notebook and a pencil. I sat up on the bed and I started to write a list. I wrote down all the things I did not like about myself.

I am untidy.

I get cross too easily.

I could not think of anything else as I sat there looking at my notebook. I got off my bed and I started to tidy my side of the room. I folded up my clothes and put them away in the wardrobe.

The wardrobe was untidy, so I took everything out and started over, folding everything neatly and putting them away again.

Then I crawled under the bed. I found two apple cores, a half a bag of sweets, a dirty towel and my missing slipper.

I made my bed, and I put my slippers on the floor beside it, just like Peanut's.

I put the bag of sweets on the windowsill so that Peanut could have some. I didn't like them anyway.

I put the towel in the laundry basket and I got back onto my tidy bed in my tidy bedroom.

I got out my list and I crossed off the first line. I was no longer untidy. I knew I would have to do it every day, but I also knew that I would. If I did it every day it would not take long.

I read the second line in my list. *I get cross too easily.* I thought about that.

Mum and Dad were cross with me all the time, but if I stopped being cross with

Bruno maybe they would stop being cross with me. Maybe I could change this too.

I was not so sure, but I decided to try.

When I was allowed out of my room, I said sorry to Bruno for hitting him.

He said, "There is still no room for you on the submarine." I did not answer. There was no submarine and I was not going to let him make me angry over something that did not exist.

"Well, if I had a submarine and there was a flood, I think I would make room for you," I lied. I would not make room for him. He was the last person I would let in my submarine.

He did not answer.

I kept out of trouble for the next two weeks. It was very difficult, but I did it. I still could not cross it off my list as I knew anything could happen. But I did try hard and I did keep my room tidy.

CHAPTER THREE

It was nearly the end of summer and we went down to the beach to swim: Bruno, Peanut and me, with Mum. There were waves that day, which made it even more fun than usual.

Peanut was in the shallow water with plastic armbands on her upper arms. She was jumping up and down in the waves. Mum was sitting on the sand watching us. Bruno and I were further out, bobbing in the waves.

"Wart," Bruno called.

I did not answer him.

Bruno and I were really good swimmers and it was such fun in the waves. I was not going to let him make me cross.

"Wart," he called again.

Up and down I bobbed. I did not even look at him.

"Susie," Bruno's voice sounded different.

I looked over to where he was, and I couldn't decide if he was just playing or not. He didn't really look like Bruno. His face was very white and I wondered how he had made himself look like that.

But he had called me "Susie".

He never called me Susie.

I swam over to him.

"Hi," I said.

"Susie, help me," Bruno said.

"Help you what?" I asked him. I was peering at his face as the waves splashed us, and I was wondering what he was doing.

"I… Susie… help…" he said.

He wasn't really swimming. The waves kept going over his head and he wasn't really doing anything.

I looked back towards the beach, and I could see Mum was standing up. But she wasn't looking at us. She was calling Peanut to come in out of the water.

"Come on," I said to Bruno. "Let's go in."

"Stay beside me," Bruno gasped.

I don't know how I did it, but somehow I pulled Bruno back towards the beach.

I wanted to shout for help but I wasn't able to swim, pull Bruno and shout all at the same time. So I forgot about the shouting and I just dragged Bruno through the water until we got closer. A man swam over and helped me. Mum was drying Peanut and she did not see.

"Are you all right?" the man said.

I couldn't reply. I was too tired. It's very difficult swimming in the waves pulling someone with you.

Bruno couldn't reply because his head kept going under the water.

The man grabbed Bruno from me.

"Keep swimming," the man said to me. He rolled over on to his back, and he held Bruno on his chest and he kicked his way back to the shore. I stayed as close as I could and we landed on the beach.

"You're all right," the man said to Bruno. "You're all right now."

Bruno sat on the sand and he coughed and spluttered and then he nodded.

"Who is with you?" the man said.

Mum came running.

"What happened?" she asked. "I took my eyes off them for just a moment. What happened?"

"This little girl just saved this boy," the man said.

I sat on the sand gasping. I hadn't really saved Bruno. The man had, but I was so tired I could hardly speak.

"Bruno, are you all right?" Mum asked. She went and got a towel and she wrapped him up. He was very white and he was shaking.

"I just got tired," he said.

I was tired too, but nobody wrapped me in a towel.

The man pulled me to my feet. "You did well," he said to me. "Are you okay now?"

I nodded. I was fine. I felt sort of frightened and excited at the same time.

Mum thanked the man. She kept thanking him as she rubbed Bruno with the towel and told me to go and get dressed.

"I didn't realise at first what was wrong," the man said to Mum. "It looked as if the little girl was rescuing the boy, but I thought they were playing. At first I thought they were playing." He kept saying the same things as though he could not quite believe what had happened.

I could not believe what had happened. Bruno is one of the best swimmers I know.

Now he was shivering and his teeth were chattering.

"I'd better get you home," Mum said. She thanked the man another six times as she hurried me to get dressed and told me to pack our things while she dried Bruno.

I put our picnic back into its basket, and I put Peanut's shoes on her feet, and I pulled on my shorts and T-shirt over my wet swimsuit. I squeezed the water out of Peanut's hair, and then I squeezed it out of mine.

Bruno had stopped shivering, but he just sat there and Mum had to help him up and into his clothes.

Peanut and I carried all our things as Mum kept her arm around Bruno as we walked back to the house.

Bruno said he was fine when we got home, but I'm not sure that he was. He just sat at the table while we ate our picnic. He didn't really say anything. He picked at a sandwich while Peanut and I tucked in.

Mum decided to put Bruno to bed. He seemed very tired. He slept all afternoon, but when he got out of bed he was still tired, so he lay in front of the television and fell asleep again.

Dad came home and they telephoned the doctor. There was something wrong with Bruno.

Bruno was sent for blood tests. And then Bruno went to hospital. Peanut and I went back to school.

The holidays were over.

CHAPTER FOUR

Bruno stayed in hospital for three months.

Peanut and I kept our room tidy and did our homework. We didn't do much else. Mum cried a lot and she and Dad spent most of their time at the hospital.

Bruno had a terrible illness.

"Did he get it in the sea?" I asked Dad when he told Peanut and me that Bruno was very sick.

"In the sea?" Dad sounded surprised.

"Yes, you remember, the day he couldn't swim in…"

"No, Susie. No, he didn't. He was already ill then, but we didn't know. It is nothing to do with the sea."

"But that was the day he got sick," I said.

Dad said, "Everyone has blood cells. Some are white and some are red. Bruno's white ones are stronger than his red ones."

"Is that bad?" Peanut asked.

"Yes, it is. But they are trying to make him better in the hospital. They are trying to make the red cells stronger."

I thought that was why he was so pale that day in the water. The white cells were fighting the red ones, and the white ones were winning. That's why he had no colour in his face.

"When is Bruno coming home?" Peanut asked.

"I don't know, Peanut," Dad said. "Not for a while."

It was easier without Bruno at home. I didn't get cross at all. There was nothing to be cross about. I crossed it off my list. But then I thought of other things to put on the list.

I will learn to swim better.

I will work harder at school.

I will help more in the house.

Peanut and I cleaned up after all our meals. Sometimes there weren't any meals. Sometimes we just had bread and butter in the evening. Sometimes we didn't see Mum for days and days. And when we did see her, her eyes were red and her face looked tired.

"Dad," I said one night before going to bed. Mum was in the hospital with Bruno.

"Yes, Susie," Dad said.

"Does Mum have the illness that Bruno has?"

He shook his head.

"Don't be silly," he said. "Of course she doesn't. Why do you think that?"

"She's in the hospital all the time with Bruno. And she is very pale like Bruno and I sort of wondered."

"Come," he said. He got up and lifted me and carried me to bed. "Mum is fine. She's just worried about Bruno."

I was worried too. I was becoming like Peanut, worrying about everything.

I worried about food because some days there was nothing in the fridge.

I worried about the weather because I needed to make sure Peanut was wrapped up going to school if it was raining.

She finished in school before me every day. She sat in the hall and waited for me so that we could walk home together. She was too little to go home alone.

Every day when we got home we went to Mrs Bird next door.

Mrs Bird had a key to our house and she let us in and settled us in the kitchen with our homework.

"There," she said. "You stay here at the table and I'll be back in to check on you in a little while."

Mrs Bird had brown curly hair. Peanut and I had curly hair too, but Mrs Bird's hair was different. It was frizzy and looked like she never brushed it. Bruno called her Mrs Bird Nest. He said she had a bird's eggs hidden in her hair and that one day they would hatch.

Peanut was worried about who would feed the birds when they hatched. She said Mrs Bird Nest might not know they were there. I did not think she could really have eggs in her hair, but Bruno said that there was a queen who had a mouse in her hair. He said if one person could have a mouse in her hair, another could have four eggs and not know it.

"Don't worry," I said to Peanut. "If Mrs Bird Nest really has eggs in her hair and they hatch, we will hear them singing and we can tell her."

During those three months while Bruno was in hospital, Mrs Bird came with us to the house every day. Sometimes she fed us, but sometimes she forgot.

"She forgets to feed us and we are real people," Peanut said. "I don't think she will remember to feed tiny birds."

I hate when Peanut worries about things. The next day I dropped my school bag under the kitchen table and I asked Mrs Bird to help me pick up my things.

When Mrs Bird bent down to help me, I waved at Peanut. I pointed to Mrs Bird's head. Peanut's eyes opened really wide when she saw what I was doing. She came over and looked at Mrs Bird's head carefully, as Mrs Bird bobbed about under the kitchen table with me.

"There's nothing there," Peanut said to me.

"I have everything," Mrs Bird said as she picked up the last pencil.

"No eggs," Peanut said in surprise.

"Sssshhhh," I whispered to Peanut.

"Eggs?" said Mrs Bird. "Do you want eggs for your tea, Peanut?"

Peanut shook her head. Ever since Bruno had said that Mrs Bird had eggs in the nest on top of her head, Peanut had not eaten an egg.

Neither had I.

One day when Peanut and I were coming home from school we went into our local shop. Peanut wanted to buy sweets. I had to buy milk and bread because we had none at home.

I paid for the food and I was putting the change away when a man said to me, "Hello. Do you remember me?"

I turned around. It was the man from the sea.

I nodded. I did remember him. We were not allowed to talk to people we did not know, but we did know this man. Sort of.

He bought Peanut and me a bar of chocolate.

"I often wondered if you were all okay," he said.

"Bruno never got better," Peanut said.

I still was not sure if we should be talking to the man, but he had saved Bruno's life.

"Bruno? He's your brother? The boy you saved?" the man said to me.

Again I nodded.

"You saved him," Peanut said to the man. "But he's been in hospital ever since then."

The man looked really confused.

"I'm sorry to hear that," he said.

He kept looking at our faces and I said to Peanut that we had to go.

We thanked him for the chocolate, said goodbye and went home.

Mrs Bird Nest let us into the house and we sat at the kitchen table while she went home. She said she had things to do and would come back to see us in a while.

I looked at Peanut.

I was wondering why the man had kept looking at us like he did. Peanut's face was dirty. I had not seen this before.

I went and looked in the mirror. My face was not much better. Since Bruno had got ill and gone to live in the hospital, nobody told us to have a bath and sometimes we forgot. My nails were dirty and so were Peanut's. And our school clothes were not very clean. Sometimes we wore the same school shirts for four or five days.

I ran a bath for Peanut. I did not like the idea that we looked dirty.

I wrote on my list in my notebook: *I will be clean and so will Peanut.*

I washed Peanut's shirt and then I washed mine. The collars were very dirty and I had to scrub them with soap.

That night when Dad came home and Peanut and I were getting ready for bed, there was a knock at the door.

Dad answered it.

I could hear voices in the hall.

"My name is John Harris," a man's voice said.

It was the man from the sea. I knew his voice.

I could hear him telling Dad that he had met us at the sea in the summer and that the woman in the local shop had given him our address.

"I came by to ask how your son is. I spoke to your daughters in the shop this afternoon, but I did not like to bother them further," he said.

Dad said, "I don't understand how you know my family."

"I was there the day the older girl saved your son's life," Mr Harris said. "I helped her pull him in, but not until she had done all the hard work."

"Oh," Dad said. His voice changed. "I did not realise who you were. We owe you a very big thank you."

"Oh, no," Mr Harris said. "As I said, the older girl did the real rescuing. I only came by because she said her brother has been in hospital ever since and I wondered what had happened."

"Bruno has cancer," Dad said.

It was difficult to hear what they were saying, but Peanut and I listened as closely as we could.

Then Mr Harris said, "My wife and I moved into a house up the road, and we would be so pleased if you and your wife and, of course, the children, came for lunch on Sunday."

CHAPTER FIVE

Mr Harris's wife was called Amanda. Dad, Peanut and I went to lunch on Sunday. Mum was in the hospital with Bruno.

Mrs Harris was beautiful. She had blonde hair and big blue eyes and a smile the size of the roast beef on the dining-room table.

"You have to call me Amanda," she said to Peanut and me. "I'm so pleased to meet you all.'

It was the nicest lunch I've ever had. Peanut said the same. We had beef and roast potatoes, peas and carrots and parsnips.

Then we had ice cream with hot chocolate sauce.

Mr Harris was a writer. He had written ten books on travel. He and Amanda had been to lots of places. He asked Dad about Bruno.

Dad talked a little about Bruno. He said he hoped Bruno would be home for Christmas.

Christmas was coming soon. There were Christmas decorations everywhere, but not in our house.

"Will we have a Christmas tree?" Peanut asked, looking at the Harris's tree. It was decorated in silver and red and had little shiny lights.

Dad sighed. "I'm not sure," he said.

"Maybe we could help," Amanda said. "Then it would be nice for Bruno when he comes home."

"I think Bruno will be in bed when he comes home," Dad said.

"We have a spare bed," Mr Harris said. "It's still in its box. We could bring it over and put it up in your living room."

"It would be no trouble," Amanda said. "We would love to help. You've had such a bad year. Let us help to make it better."

I thought Dad was going to say no, but instead he said, "You're so kind. I can't thank you enough."

"We're very short on time," Dad then said. "We spend so much time in the hospital. There really has been no time for thinking about Christmas or presents or anything."

"I can imagine," Mr Harris said.

"I know," Amanda said. "John and I would love to bring Susie and Peanut in to see Santa. Would that be all right?" she asked Dad.

I thought Dad was going to start crying. He could not speak. Neither could Peanut or I.

"We would love to," Mr Harris said.

"Oh, Dad, please," Peanut said.

Dad nodded his head.

"This is so kind of you. The girls have not had much fun lately. I'm so grateful."

Peanut and I were grateful too.

Mr Harris drove us into town. Amanda held my hand and Mr Harris held Peanut's as we walked from the car to the shops. All the windows were full of lights and Christmas presents. We kept stopping to look at different things. When we came to the shop where Santa was waiting in his grotto, we saw wonderful toys. I saw a doll that looked a bit like Amanda with yellow hair and blue eyes. She was the most beautiful doll I had ever seen.

I touched her hair.

Mr Harris said, "She's a lovely doll."

"She's so pretty," I said. "She looks like Amanda."

He agreed and Amanda laughed.

Peanut saw an ark with lots of tiny animals and Noah and little birds. You had to build the ark from little pieces that locked into each other.

And then we went in to see Santa.

Peanut sat on his knee and he said to her, "What would you like for Christmas?"

She told him about the ark and he said he would see what he could do.

Then he asked me what I would like. I wanted to tell him about the doll that looked like Amanda, but suddenly I thought of Bruno and Mum and Dad and the cancer and all the sadness from the last few months.

"Can you make my brother better?" I asked Santa.

He slipped Peanut down from his knee and he let me sit there instead. He had a big white beard and white eyebrows and a very nice smile.

"What's your name?" He asked me.

"I'm Susie," I told him.

"And are these your parents?" he asked, looking at Mr Harris and Amanda.

I shook my head.

"Mum and Dad are in the hospital with my brother," I said.

"He's been there for three months," Peanut said.

"Three months is a long time," Santa said.

"It's more than that really," I said. "It's three months, two weeks and four days."

Santa nodded. I think he knew that that was a very long time. In all that time Peanut and I had not seen Bruno. We were not allowed to visit him because of infections. Dad had said to us that any infection would be very bad for Bruno.

"His white blood cells are fighting his red ones," I told Santa. "I'm not sure which are winning."

I often thought of Bruno that day in the sea and how he was suddenly not able to fight the waves. I was very worried that he would not be able to fight the white cells.

"There are some presents I can't always give," Santa said.

Peanut looked worried. She put her hand on Santa's other knee.

"Would you try?" she asked.

"I'll try," he said.

Mr Harris said, "We're hoping Bruno will be home for Christmas."

Santa nodded. "You're very good little girls," he said to Peanut and me.

After we left Santa, Mr Harris and Amanda took us to lunch. Peanut and I had the nicest soup and warm bread that smelled as good as it tasted. Then Amanda said we would go home on the bus as Mr Harris had some things to do in town.

It was very cold walking to the bus stop and Amanda brought us into a shop and bought us gloves and scarves and woolly hats. Peanut chose hers in pink. Mine were white.

"Are you sure?" I asked Amanda. I wasn't sure that Mum and Dad would like us taking things like this.

"Sure about what?" asked Amanda.

"About buying us these," I said, touching my hat.

"It's an early Christmas present," Amanda said. "In my family we always give early Christmas presents."

That sounded good, so Peanut and I thanked her. The lady in the shop cut off the price tags, and Peanut and I put on our new hats and scarves. Peanut looked so pretty with her hair curling out under her hat and Amanda gave us each a kiss. "You're the best children I've ever met," she said. She had tears in her eyes. I don't know why. Peanut and I felt really lucky. Peanut was smiling and didn't look at all worried.

On the bus home I thought about how nice Mr Harris and Amanda were.

I said to Amanda, "Thank you for bringing us into town, Amanda. You and Mr Harris are so kind to Peanut and me."

"It's nice to be kind," Amanda said. "We love doing things for you. It makes us happy. We don't have any children, so it's lovely for us to bring you to see Santa."

But I didn't mean just bringing us to see Santa. I meant the whole thing. I meant lunch, and the woolly hats, and the bed for Bruno. And letting Peanut and me taste Christmas the way we just had. I meant the fact that she had made Peanut smile and that she held our hands and that she and Mr Harris had made those dark days change.

That night they helped put up the Christmas tree. Then Dad and Mr Harris put the bed together. The living room looked lovely and friendly and I knew that Bruno was going to be pleased when he came home.

CHAPTER SIX

Bruno came home on Christmas Eve. He was all wrapped up in a coat and hat and he had a blanket around him. Peanut and I were watching from the bedroom window as Mum and Dad helped him out of the car. Dad had asked us to stay in the bedroom until they got Bruno into the house.

Peanut and I held hands. We waited until Mum came and said we could come in to see Bruno.

We went into the living room where the Christmas tree was looking so pretty. There was someone in the Harris's bed. We both looked at the person. Then we looked again. Then Peanut suddenly sat down on the floor and didn't move.

The person in the bed was Bruno. He had no eyebrows and no hair on his head, but it was Bruno. I was almost sure. I went closer and looked at him.

"Hah," said the person in the bed.

It was Bruno. Bruno always said "hah".

Peanut still did not move from the floor, where she was sitting with her mouth open.

I went closer and I said, "Hi Bruno."

Bruno said "hah," again.

Peanut got up off the floor and came over too.

"Hi Bruno," she said. Her voice was very weak. I could see she was not quite sure if it was Bruno.

"We're glad you're home, Bruno," I said firmly, so Peanut would know it was all right. "Look, we put up the tree," I said, to give Peanut time to think of something to say.

"Hah," said Bruno again. "It looks great."

"Can I touch your head?" Peanut asked.

"Yes," Bruno said.

"You don't have any hair," Peanut said. I was pretty sure that Bruno already knew that. She stroked his head.

"It feels nice and smooth," Peanut said.

"It will grow back in a while," Bruno said to her. "It all fell out because of the medicine I had to take."

"Were you very sick?" Peanut asked.

"Yes," said Bruno. "But I'm pretty much better now."

Then he suddenly closed his eyes and fell asleep.

Dad and Mum had a glass of wine in front of the fire by the Christmas tree. Peanut and I sat with them for a while and then we went to bed.

Mum came to tuck us in.

"I'm glad you're home," Peanut said.

We had only seen Mum about ten times since Bruno went to hospital. It was so nice that she was back. She looked happier than she had in ages.

"It's good to be home," she said.

It was good. Good that both she and Bruno were home. Good that she was able to smile at us.

I wondered what would go wrong next.

We knew there would be no Christmas presents because Dad and Mum had had no time. They had said that our Christmas present was that the family was back together. I thought that was a good enough present.

But Santa did come.

When we got up in the morning and went in to see Bruno, Santa's presents were under the tree.

Peanut got the ark she had seen in the shop in town. Bruno got a Spiderman outfit. I got the beautiful doll that looked like

Amanda. There were books and chocolates and all kinds of nice things.

"Oh, Santa is wonderful," Peanut said, gasping in joy.

"Santa is very, very good," Mum said.

"There is real goodness out there," Dad said holding Mum's hand.

Bruno was sitting up in bed and he looked much better.

I loved my doll. I named her Mandy and I combed her hair. I changed her clothes. There was a little bag that she had, and in it were two other dresses and clips for her hair and all kinds of things like socks and shoes and a hat. She was the most beautiful doll I had ever seen. And she was mine.

I made her a bed out of a shoebox and I put my white woolly scarf in it. Then I laid Mandy in it. When she was lying down, her eyes closed. When she was sitting up, they opened.

She was a bit like Bruno. Every time he lay down on his pillows he closed his eyes and went to sleep. When he sat up his eyes were open. When he looked tired, Mum went over to him and she helped him lie back on the pillow. I did the same with Mandy. I kissed her and I stroked her. I loved her yellow hair.

There was still no sign of any hair on Bruno's head. I wondered when it would come back.

On Christmas night after we had all gone to bed, I could not sleep. I wondered how Bruno was feeling, so I decided I would go into the living room.

He was lying there in the new bed and he was looking at the Christmas tree. The fire had died down and the guard was in front of it.

"Hello," I said to him.

"Hah," he replied.

"What are you doing?" I asked.

"Nothing," he said. "Just looking."

"The tree is lovely, isn't it?" I said. "Mr Harris and Amanda helped us to put it up."

"I know," he said. "Dad and Mum told me."

"Do you remember Mr Harris?" I asked Bruno.

"No," he said.

"He's the man who rescued you in the sea."

"You saved me, Susie," Bruno said.

"I didn't really," I told him. "I wasn't strong enough. I could only bring you so far."

"It was far enough," he said. "When I was really ill in hospital, I wished once that you had not saved me. But now I'm glad you did."

It's funny how you forget things. I remember that I was really upset when Bruno stuck the knife in my hand. And I remember being really angry when he ruined my apple-green dress and my beautiful chocolate cake. But I couldn't feel that upset or that anger any more. They were gone. I just felt glad that Bruno was home and that he could see the Christmas tree and the fire, and that he had eaten a little of the Christmas dinner.

"Hey, Susie," Bruno said.

"What is it?" I asked. I was kneeling on the floor by the fire because the room was getting cold.

"Would you read to me?" he asked.

I was so surprised. Bruno never asked for things like that. I got one of his books and I sat near the tree where there was enough light. I began to read aloud.

I read until he fell asleep. Then I read a little bit more in case he was not really asleep. But then I could hear his breathing. It was very quiet and even, and I knew that Bruno really was asleep.

I went back to bed. I was very cold.

CHAPTER SEVEN

Every night after that when Mum, Dad and Peanut had gone to sleep, I went back in to Bruno and I read to him.

One night while I was reading, Bruno said, "I wish my hair would grow back."

I looked at him. "Dad said it will grow back soon," I said.

"I know. But I'm glad I'm not going back to school yet," Bruno said. "I know I would be teased."

"For having no hair?" I asked.

It seemed very mean to me that anyone would laugh at Bruno for having no hair.

"Yes," he said, touching his head.

After he fell asleep I sat there looking at him. I was thinking that life isn't always very fair. Even though Bruno had been mean to me in the past, he had never done anything to deserve this.

I turned out the light and I went and got Mandy.

I brought her to the bathroom, and, with Dad's razor, I shaved off all her hair. Then I cut off her eyelashes. She had no real eyebrows. They were painted on to her face. Then I went to bed.

When I woke up I had forgotten what I had done. It was Sunday and Mr Harris and Amanda were coming to lunch.

They hugged Peanut and me. Then they went to say hello to Bruno.

"We're so pleased to meet you, Bruno," Mr Harris said, shaking his hand.

"It's lovely that you are home at last," said Amanda.

Bruno said, "Hah." Then he said, "I got a Spiderman outfit for Christmas."

"And I got an ark," Peanut said. Peanut's ark was on the floor, and she had all the tiny animals in pairs in front of it. Mr and Mrs Noah were standing on the deck of the ark.

"And what did you get, Susie?" Mr Harris asked.

"Bring your doll in," Mum said to me.

As I walked to the bedroom I remembered what I had done to Mandy during the night. I lifted her out of her shoebox and I hugged her. I did not know what to do. If I brought her inside they would all see what I had done. She was wearing her blue dress and white socks. I pulled on her little black shoes, and then I put her hat on her head. With the hat on, she looked almost perfect. I hoped they would not notice that she had no eyelashes.

I did not want to bring her back in to the living room. I had a bad feeling. I went really slowly. When I brought her in everyone was having a drink and Bruno was laughing at something. Peanut was lying on the floor with her ark.

I stood in the doorway hoping no one would see me and Mandy.

"Come on in," Mum said. "Show John and Amanda what Santa brought you."

I came in slowly, trying to keep a smile on my face. I held Mandy close so they could not really see her.

"I love her," I said, hugging her tight.

"Show them," Mum said again.

I had no choice. I had to let them see her a little.

"She's asleep," I said, holding her flat so that her eyes would stay closed. She looked worse like that so I held her upright and her eyes opened.

Mum took a closer look.

"Let me see," she said. She took Mandy from me and she looked at her face. Then she pulled off the hat and she stared in horror.

"Susie, what have you done?" she asked. Her voice was angry. "What have you done?" she asked again.

I didn't know what to say. I could not explain why I had done it. I was not even sure I knew why I had done it. I opened and closed my mouth but I could not think of a single thing to say.

"Susie, how could you?" Mum said. Now her voice was really angry. How could you do that to the doll Mr Harris and Amanda gave you?"

"Santa gave it to me," I said. I knew I was going to cry. I could feel the tears in my eyes and my voice sounded funny.

"Go to your room at once," Mum said.

The tears poured down my face. I grabbed Mandy from Mum and I ran back to my room. I lay on my bed and I cried and cried.

I cried because nothing was the same any more. I cried because Bruno had nearly died in the sea and then he went away to hospital. I cried because Peanut and I were always alone. I cried because we were sometimes hungry and Mrs Bird Nest forgot to feed us. I cried because I felt no one loved me any more. And I cried for Mandy. I loved her and I had shaved off all her hair.

Suddenly I felt someone sitting on the bed beside me. It was Amanda and she lifted me up into her arms.

"It's all right," she whispered. "It's all right now, Susie. Don't cry."

I had to stop crying to hear her because she was talking so quietly.

"I don't know why I did it," I said to her. I was still sobbing a bit. "When I did it, I had a reason, but I can't really remember."

"Was it to do with Bruno?" she asked me. I nodded.

"He told me that he was glad he wasn't going back to school because he had no hair and he would be teased," I said.

Amanda listened.

"I thought that if I shaved off Mandy's hair he would see that I still loved her. He would see that she was still my beautiful doll even if she had no hair. I did not do it to hurt Mandy. I love her."

"I understand," Amanda said to me. She was stroking my hair. Then she wiped my face and she kissed my forehead. "Now, let's dry those eyes," she said. "Everything is going to be all right."

When I had really stopped crying, Amanda brushed my hair. She washed my face and she told me again that everything was going to be all right.

She took me by the hand and we went to look for Mum and Dad. They were in the kitchen with Mr Harris.

"Susie has something to tell you," Amanda said.

Did I? I could not think what she meant.

"Go on, Susie," Amanda said. "I want you to tell them what you told me."

I looked at her. I looked at Mum who was looking cross. I looked at Dad who was looking confused. I looked at Mr Harris and he smiled gently at me. Amanda kept her hand on my shoulder. Her hand felt strong and safe.

I still could not think what to say. It all sounded so silly.

"Tell them why you shaved Mandy's head," Amanda said. "Tell them what Bruno said."

I took a deep breath.

"Bruno told me that he was afraid he would be teased because he has lost all his hair. I thought that if he could see that I still love Mandy with no hair then he would not feel so bad."

It sounded stupid. I felt stupid.

Big tears ran down Mum's cheeks.

"When did he say that?" she asked.

I had not meant to make her cry.

"During the night when I was reading to him," I said.

Dad put his arms around Mum.

Mr Harris patted my head.

Then Mum came over and she put her arms around me.

"Oh, Susie," she said. "I'm sorry I was angry with you. I didn't understand."

Then I started crying again. Dad hugged us both.

When we had stopped hugging and crying, I realised both Mr Harris and Amanda had gone.

When we went back into the living room, they were there with Bruno and Peanut.

CHAPTER EIGHT

"John and I have had an idea," Amanda said.

Mr Harris nodded. I wondered what their idea was.

"When Susie and Peanut go back to school, we thought that maybe I could collect them every day until Bruno is fully better. It would give you time with Bruno," Amanda said to Mum.

"They could come back to our house to do their homework."

"Oh," Mum said. "That is very kind of you."

I was not sure if she had agreed or not.

"It would make life a lot easier," Dad said slowly. "This is really very nice of you."

"Bruno has to go in and out of hospital for a couple of weeks," Mum said. I could see she was thinking about the offer Mr Harris and Amanda had made.

"We would be happy for them to stay over on nights when it is difficult for you," Amanda said.

"Could we eat with you?" Peanut asked hopefully. "Mrs Bird Nest sometimes forgets to feed us."

"What?" said Dad in surprise. "She doesn't feed you? Mrs Bird? But I pay her to look after you and to feed you."

"She forgets," I said.

"Why didn't you tell me?" Dad asked.

"We didn't want to worry you," I said.

"You told us not to worry you," Peanut said. "You said there are enough problems with Bruno being sick."

Dad shook his head.

"I'm shocked," he said. "I paid Mrs Bird to look after you."

"Well, if you let us look after Susie and Peanut you won't have to worry," Mr Harris said. "We won't forget to feed them."

I said, "Please, Mum."

Peanut said, "Please, Mum."

Bruno said, "Hah."

Mum and Dad agreed.

That night I got up when everyone was asleep, and I went in to Bruno. He was lying there looking at the tree. I got a book to read to him.

"Susie," Bruno said.

"Yes," I answered as I turned the pages, trying to find where I had finished reading the night before.

"Why did you shave off Mandy's hair?"

"I don't know," I said as I found the right place in the book.

"It won't grow back," he said.

"I know."

"My hair will grow back," he said.

I nodded.

"I like her with hair or without hair," I said. "She's still the same doll. And I love her."

"Hah," said Bruno.

I began to read.

Bruno fell asleep after about five minutes. I stayed by the fire for a while.

That winter, while Bruno was getting better, Peanut and I spent our afternoons at the Harris's house. We did our homework at the kitchen table and Amanda made us hot chocolate. We had dinner in the evenings with them and then Dad collected us.

Twice we stayed over while Bruno was in hospital.

"How is Bruno?" Mr Harris asked one evening at dinner.

"His hair is growing back," I said.

"He says he's going to be a doctor when he grows up," Peanut said.

"He's going to make sick children better," I said.

"I'm going to be a vet," Peanut said. "I'm going to work in an ark."

"What do you want to do when you grow up?" Amanda asked me.

"I'm going to write books like Mr Harris," I said.

"That's great," Mr Harris said. "Have you written anything yet?"

I nodded. In my little notebook, where once I had written how I was going to change myself, to be tidy, and nice, and good, I had written a story.

It was not yet finished because I wanted to wait until Bruno was better.

"May I see it?" Mr Harris asked.

"It's not finished yet," I said.

"What's it about?" Amanda asked as she served the potatoes. We were having fish and peas and a lovely sauce. Amanda cooked beautiful food and Peanut and I were never hungry.

"It's about us," I said. "It's about how things change. It's about being happy again."

I was happy again. That was the truth. I had been really sad. Peanut had been really worried. Now we were not like that any more.

Since Bruno had started getting better, Dad and Mum were happier too. Dad said that Bruno's illness had made him enjoy life more. That was true too.

He and Mum were still busy with Bruno and the hospital, but when they were at home there was more time for Peanut and me.

Bruno did not fight with me any more. He called me Susie and not Wart. He and I were kinder to each other. Sometimes I still read to him late at night, but he was sleeping better. Also he read to himself again. He did not need me like he had when he was really ill.

"When you have finished writing your book, I would love to read it," Mr Harris said.

"I would too," Amanda said.

"What's it called?" Peanut asked.

It was the story of three children and what had happened to them one year, how their lives changed when one of them became ill and how they learned to support each other instead of fighting.

It was a story of love and kindness.

It was called *Bruno, Peanut and Me*.